BLEAK HOUSE

Written by **Charles Dickens**
Illustrations by **Jon Davis**

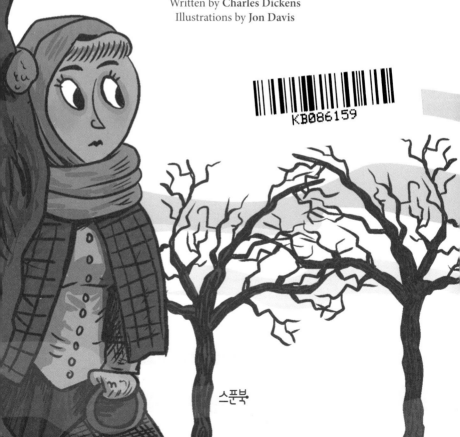

스푼북

ESTHER

There was once a young girl called Esther Summerson. Esther had never known her mother or father. She lived with Miss Barbary, her aunt. Miss Barbary was a horribly strict woman, who never smiled or spoke kindly to Esther.

Esther had a lot of questions about her parents. Her aunt never answered them. She only mentioned Esther's mother once, on Esther's birthday. Miss Barbary told Esther that it would have been better if she hadn't been born. She said Esther's mother was a disgrace. 'An utter disgrace!' she shouted at Esther. 'You should forget all about your useless parents.'

Esther was miserable and
lonely. She didn't often meet other
children. Even when she did, her
aunt forbade her from playing
with them.

The only friend Esther had in the world was her doll. Sometimes she would cry herself to sleep, holding the doll to her cheek.

Esther also had a little white handkerchief. It had the letters H.B. embroidered on it in blue thread. She treasured it because she believed it once belonged to her mother.

Then, one day, everything changed.

When Esther was fourteen, her aunt died suddenly. A kind man called John Jarndyce became her guardian. He sent Esther to a boarding school. Here, for the first time in her life, Esther made friends. She was happy.

After six joyful years at school, Esther received a letter. Mr Jarndyce wanted her to come and stay at his house in the country. It was called Bleak House. Esther was worried it would live up to its name.

Mr Jarndyce was also the guardian to two other young people: Ada Clare and Richard Carstone. They were very distant members of his family. He wanted them to come to Bleak House as well.

Esther, Ada and Richard met in London, before travelling together to Mr Jarndyce's home.

Ada had thick golden hair and soft blue eyes. She was very friendly. Esther soon felt as if they had known each other for a long time.

Richard was nice, too. He was a cheerful young man who didn't take life too seriously.

It was a cold, frosty evening when the three finally arrived. The house they were travelling to lay just outside the town of St Albans. But Bleak House didn't look bleak at all. Candlelight sparkled from its windows and warmth spilled out of the front door.

Their guardian, John Jarndyce, was there to greet them. He couldn't have been more welcoming.

'Ada, my love, Esther, my dear, you are welcome here,' said Mr Jarndyce. He hugged them. 'I am so happy to see you! Richard, if I had a hand to spare, I would shake yours!'

John Jarndyce was a silver-haired
man, with a face full of kindness. Like
its owner, his house was warm and
welcoming, and certainly *not* bleak.

But John Jarndyce explained that
it had once been bleak indeed.

Bleak House had been left to John
by an uncle, Tom Jarndyce. This uncle

had spent his life fighting in a legal case called Jarndyce and Jarndyce. This case was many, many years old.

The Jarndyce and Jarndyce case was about a will. A long time ago, someone called Jarndyce had left a lot of money to someone else called Jarndyce. But a third person in the Jarndyce family claimed *he* ought to have the money. Then a fourth person said the same thing, and then a fifth, and a sixth, and so on …

The argument had gone on for so many years that no one could remember how it started.

Lawyers argued. Different lawyers made different arguments. Judges made judgements. Different judges made different judgements.

Everyone went round and round in circles.

The case was never-ending. But some members of the Jarndyce family still hoped that one day *they* might get the money.

Old Tom Jarndyce spent his whole life reading legal papers. He went to court again and again. The court was in the middle of London, so he travelled a lot. Meanwhile, Bleak House was falling to pieces.

The wind whistled through the cracked walls, and rain fell through the roof.

After Tom died, John Jarndyce started to put things right. He had the roof and walls repaired. He turned Bleak House into a cheerful, welcoming home.

John had a word of advice for his young wards, Ada, Richard and Esther.

'Never get involved in the Jarndyce and Jarndyce case. It is a curse, not a blessing. It will destroy your lives.'

LADY
DEDLOCK

Lady Dedlock was involved with the Jarndyce and Jarndyce case. She and her husband, Sir Leicester Dedlock, owned a house in the countryside. It was much larger and grander than Bleak House.

The only problem was that Lady Dedlock found the countryside very boring. There was nothing to do there. Especially when it was stormy and wet. The Dedlocks spent days sitting and watching the rain. Finally, they'd had enough. 'We simply must go back to London,' moaned Lady Dedlock to her husband. 'I cannot watch another raindrop run down another windowpane – I'll go mad!'

And so, they went. Sir Leicester and Lady Dedlock travelled to their house in London. There, there was more excitement. One day, a lawyer called Mr Tulkinghorn came to see them. He had some information he wanted to show the Dedlocks. Mr Tulkinghorn was a hard-faced, sharp-nosed man. He worked on the Jarndyce and Jarndyce case. He also liked finding out secrets about the important people he worked for. Knowing their secrets gave him power over them, and he *loved* power.

It was a cold, wet, gloomy

afternoon and Lady Dedlock sat on a sofa by the fire. She wasn't interested in what Mr Tulkinghorn had to say. She glanced lazily over at the papers he had brought with him.

Lady Dedlock's blood ran cold. She thought she recognised one of the handwritten papers lying on a table nearby. It couldn't be, could it? She stood up.

'Who wrote that?' she asked Mr Tulkinghorn.

'I don't know,' replied the lawyer. 'There are men paid to copy out these documents. They are called law-writers. Why do you ask, my lady?'

Lady Dedlock waved an elegant hand in the air as if to show her question didn't matter. The rings on her hand sparkled in the firelight.

She sat back down.

But the question did matter.

Mr Tulkinghorn saw how Lady Dedlock's eyes kept darting back to the paper on the table. It was obvious to Mr Tulkinghorn that Lady Dedlock recognised the handwriting.

Suddenly, the colour drained from Lady Dedlock's face. She said she thought she might faint. Sir Leicester summoned Hortense, her maid, who helped her to bed.

Lady Dedlock's husband was worried about his wife. He didn't notice anything odd about the way she had acted though. He was much older than her and his sight and his hearing weren't so sharp.

As they finished their meeting, Mr Tulkinghorn couldn't help thinking about what had happened. It was clear that Lady Dedlock had a secret, and he liked collecting secrets. He decided to find out who had copied out the legal document that she was so curious about.

MR TULKINGHORN INVESTIGATES

Mr Tulkinghorn went to the office where his legal papers were copied. He discovered that the work had been done by someone called Nemo.

Nemo?

That was strange. Nemo was the Latin word for 'nobody'.

Mr Tulkinghorn learned that Nemo lived close by. He rented a room above a junk shop. It was nighttime by now, but Mr Tulkinghorn was determined to visit the man.

Who was he? And why had Lady
Dedlock reacted so strangely to the
sight of his handwriting?

The owner of the junk shop, Mr
Krook, told Mr Tulkinghorn that
he hardly ever saw Nemo.

'Shall I call him down, sir? I don't think he'll answer though. He might as well be dead. He keeps himself to himself, does Mr Nemo.'

'I'll go up to him then,' replied Mr Tulkinghorn.

'Second floor, sir. It's dark up there. Take this candle.'

Mr Tulkinghorn nodded and went up the narrow stairs. He reached the dark door on the second floor.

He knocked.

No answer.

He opened the door, and accidentally blew out his candle in doing so.

The small room was almost
black with soot and dirt. A candle
burnt low on a broken desk. Mr
Tulkinghorn could also see a couple
of chairs and a low bed.

There was a man lying on the
bed. He was dressed in a dirty shirt
and ragged trousers, with bare feet.
His hair and beard were tangled.

A couple of empty bottles lay on the floor next to the bed.

'Hello, my friend!' shouted Mr Tulkinghorn, banging his iron candlestick against the door.

The man did not move and did not answer.

Mr Tulkinghorn shouted again.

Still the man on the bed did not move, and still he did not answer.

Mr Tulkinghorn called for a doctor but it was too late.

Nemo was dead.

He was not old, but drink and poverty had hastened his death. Mr Krook, Nemo's landlord, complained that the dead man owed him six weeks' rent.

Only one person seemed sorry about Nemo's death. He was a young lad called Jo. Jo couldn't read or write and he slept on the streets. He earned a small amount of money from rich ladies, who would pay him to sweep the roads before they crossed them. Nemo had been kind to Jo. Even though he had almost no money himself, he would always give a penny or two to the boy. Now Jo sobbed. He wished he'd told Nemo just how much his help had meant.

Mr Tulkinghorn stood by and watched.

He wondered again why Lady Dedlock was so startled to see Nemo's handwriting.

Mr Tulkinghorn would have wondered even more if he had seen what happened a few weeks later.

One evening, a woman found Jo the sweeper sitting in a shop doorway. She asked the lad about his friend, the man called Nemo. Jo was a little frightened. He couldn't see the woman's face beneath her hat and her veil. He could only hear her soft voice. She certainly sounded like a lady but she was dressed in plain clothes, like a servant.

She said she would pay Jo to
take her to the house where Nemo
had died. Then she asked to see the

place where he was buried.

The cemetery was in a poor part of London, behind a barred gate.

She gazed through the bars of the gate and sighed. When she took off her gloves to get the money from her purse, Jo noticed how clean and small her hands were. He noticed the fine rings that sparkled on her fingers. *Strange kind of servant*, he thought.

Lady Dedlock and Esther

One day, Sir Leicester and Lady Dedlock were visiting friends in the country. They were staying close to Bleak House. Lady Dedlock went for a walk with her maid, Hortense.

All at once, a violent thunderstorm broke out. Lightning flashed, thunder rolled and the rain came plunging down.

Luckily, there was an empty cottage nearby. Lady Dedlock and Hortense took shelter under the porch of the cottage. After a moment, three more people ran in to join them.

It was John Jarndyce and his wards, Ada and Esther. They too had got caught in the storm.

Mr Jarndyce already knew Lady Dedlock. He introduced his wards to her. Lady Dedlock told Ada how pretty she was. Then, she turned to Esther. 'Have you really lost both of your parents, Miss Summerson?' she asked.

'I never knew my parents,' Esther replied.

For some reason, Esther found it difficult to speak. Her heart was beating fast and her voice sounded distant in her own ears. A strange look passed over Lady Dedlock's face. She turned and started talking to Mr Jarndyce.

All the time, Hortense watched Lady Dedlock and Esther very carefully.

When the storm was over and they were back in Bleak House, Esther saw Ada glancing curiously at her. She asked why.

'Oh, it's nothing,' said Ada. 'It's

just that I couldn't help noticing that you and Lady Dedlock – well, Esther, you look quite like her.'

Esther was so surprised that she almost forgot to laugh.

46

After all, what connection could there be between a simple young woman like herself and a grand lady?

Ada Clare quickly brushed off the idea after that. She had other things to think about. She and Richard Carstone had fallen in love and were planning to get married. John

Jarndyce approved. He was very fond of his two wards and wanted to see them happy. But he was worried about Richard.

'The trouble with Richard,' he said to Esther, 'is that he can't seem to settle down. He pins all his hopes on the idea that one day he will win money from the Jarndyce and Jarndyce case. Like my uncle Tom, he is looking forward to getting rich.'

'You don't think that will happen?' said Esther.

'The only people who make money out of the Jarndyce and Jarndyce case are the lawyers,' muttered John Jarndyce. 'It brings ruin to everybody else.'

Lady Dedlock and Mr Tulkinghorn

In the meantime, Mr Tulkinghorn continued his investigation into the mysterious Nemo. He had made some discoveries. It was time to visit Lady Dedlock. Mr Tulkinghorn walked into the Dedlocks' house and stood to face Lady Dedlock. She was sitting in a chair by the fire. He towered over her. Mr Tulkinghorn was tall, and all dressed in black.

With his sharp nose and furrowed
brow, he looked like a bird of prey.

'I have a question, my lady,' he
began. Did you once know an officer
in the British Army called Captain
James Hawdon?'

Lady Dedlock raised her hand to her mouth. The rings on her fingers sparkled in the firelight.

She nodded.

'Captain Hawdon fell on hard times and turned to drink. In the end he became what is called a law-writer. He was so ashamed of what he'd become that he hid away and called himself Nemo.'

'I did not know that, Mr Tulkinghorn,' Lady Dedlock replied. She was trying to stay calm. But the lawyer heard a tremble in her voice.

'That was true *once*, Lady Dedlock,' he said, 'but you recognised Captain Hawdon's handwriting in the papers I showed you a few months ago. Am I wrong?' He gave her a stern look.

'I loved him,' said Lady Dedlock simply. 'I loved James Hawdon.'

Mr Tulkinghorn told her how he'd tracked down Jo the sweeper. He'd heard all about the lady with the veil who wished to see where Nemo was buried.

'I believe that lady with the veil was you, my lady. You were dressed in your maid Hortense's clothes.'

'You know everything,' said Lady Dedlock with a sigh.

Mr Tulkinghorn did know everything. He had paid Hortense to spy on Lady Dedlock.

'You had a child with Captain Hawdon,' Mr Tulkinghorn went on. 'What happened to it?'

'I was very young,' said Lady Dedlock. 'My sister, Anne Barbary, was there. I was very ill at the time, and my little girl died hours after her birth. My sister judged me for having a child without being married. She told me that I was a disgrace. We stopped talking, and now she is dead too.'

'But your daughter is alive,' said Mr Tulkinghorn.

Lady Dedlock gasped.

'Your sister looked after her until her death, and she lives with Mr John Jarndyce. He is her guardian. Her name is Esther Summerson.'

Lady Dedlock remembered meeting Esther during the thunderstorm.

'Why are you telling me all this?' she asked.

'Don't you think a mother ought to know her own daughter?' said Mr Tulkinghorn. Then a wicked glint sparkled in his eye. 'And should Sir Leicester Dedlock be told the secrets of your past?'

'Don't tell him,' begged Lady Dedlock. 'The shock would kill him.'

'We shall see,' said Mr Tulkinghorn.

He turned and stalked from the room like a great, evil bird of prey.

Lady Dedlock and Esther

Esther Summerson had been very ill. John Jarndyce and Ada had been very worried for her. But now, finally, she was getting better.

Esther was out walking near Bleak House. She climbed a slope and sat down on a bench to look at the sunlit fields and woods. A figure was coming towards her. She was surprised to recognise Lady Dedlock.

'Miss Summerson, I am afraid I
have startled you,' said Lady Dedlock.
'I heard that you have been very ill.'

Lady Dedlock's face was pale. She
sat down beside Esther and took
her hand.

'My dear girl, I have something to tell you …' began Lady Dedlock, but she could not go on. Her eyes filled with tears. As she dabbed them away, Esther noticed that Lady Dedlock's white handkerchief had the letters H.B. embroidered on it in blue thread. It looked just like Esther's handkerchief. She always kept it because it had been her mother's.

Esther looked at Lady Dedlock, but could not see her through her own tears. She could hardly breathe.

Esther and Lady Dedlock hugged each other.

After a time, Lady Dedlock told Esther about her father, Captain James Hawdon. How they had been deeply in love when they were very young. How her family had disapproved. How she and James Hawdon had separated. How she had given birth to a baby girl.

How she had been told that her daughter was dead.

Instead, the baby, Esther, had been taken away and looked after by her sister, Anne Barbary.

Lady Dedlock had been Honoria Barbary.

H.B.

Then she became Lady Dedlock, a rich woman with grand houses in the country and in London. Her husband, Sir Leicester Dedlock, was old and respectable. He loved her but he knew nothing of her past life.

She had thought her past was dead and buried. That was before she saw the handwriting which she recognised as James Hawdon's, Esther's father.

Esther could hardly take all this in.

Before Esther could respond, Lady Dedlock told her that they had to part. Something had happened. A man called Mr Tulkinghorn knew her secret, and he was going to tell her husband. Sir Leicester would never forgive her.

She didn't know what to do. She might have to leave England forever.

Esther tried to persuade her to stay, but her mother gave her a final hug and a final kiss. Then she walked away.

Mr Tulkinghorn

Mr Tulkinghorn was enjoying his power. He was playing with Lady Dedlock like a cat plays with a mouse. If he revealed her past, he could ruin the lives of everyone around her. Would he do it or not? That would depend on what Lady Dedlock did.

The lawyer went to see Lady Dedlock. He wanted to scare her – if she thought he was going to reveal her secret, she would give him anything he wanted. When he arrived outside the grand house, one of Lady Dedlock's maids was leaving with packed bags. Mr Tulkinghorn was furious. The Lady was getting rid of people so he had less spies to watch her.

He marched into the house.

'I do not approve,' he said angrily, 'of what you are doing. I see that you are trying to wriggle out of this situation.'

'Why shouldn't I?' said Lady Dedlock.

'Because now you have forced me to reveal the secret you are trying to escape,' replied Mr Tulkinghorn. 'You cannot escape me.' With that, the lawyer turned on his heels and left.

Later that night, Mr Tulkinghorn was working in his office. Hortense, Lady Dedlock's maid, had been to visit him. Now Mr Tulkinghorn had found out Lady Dedlock's secrets, he did not need Hortense. He wasn't going to pay her any more.

She was angry.

Hortense had a fierce temper. She shouted until Mr Tulkinghorn made her leave. She stormed out of Mr Tulkinghorn's office and stamped her way downstairs.

It was a very quiet night. There was a brilliant moon. Its light turned the church steeples and rooftops of London into silver.

If you had been walking outside Mr Tulkinghorn's office just before ten o'clock that night, you would have heard the BANG of a gun being fired. And if you had opened the door and walked up the stairs to Mr Tulkinghorn's office you would not have seen him at his desk. He lay face down on the floor. He had been shot straight through the heart.

Mr Bucket
Investigates

There was a police inspector in London named Bucket. It was a rather strange name but it suited the inspector. He was solid and round, just like a bucket, and he liked to scoop up pieces of information.

Inspector Bucket was investigating the murder of Mr Tulkinghorn.

Some unknown person had sent him a letter. It said: 'Lady Dedlock, murderer'.

But Inspector Bucket didn't believe everything he saw or read. He thought very carefully about things.

He visited Sir Leicester Dedlock, because Mr Tulkinghorn had been Sir Leicester's lawyer.

Inspector Bucket told Sir Leicester everything he'd found out about his wife's past. How she'd been in love with a young captain. How she'd had a baby without being married, and how she'd believed her child was dead. Sir Leicester was horrified to hear how much his wife had suffered.

And now she was gone. She had run away.

Inspector Bucket thought for a while. That was suspicious. Perhaps Lady Dedlock *was* the murderer.

Then Inspector Bucket interviewed Hortense, Lady Dedlock's former maid.

Hortense admitted that she knew Mr Tulkinghorn, but did not say he'd paid her to spy on her mistress. Inspector Bucket noticed that Hortense grew angry when she mentioned Mr Tulkinghorn.

The gunshot that had killed Mr

Tulkinghorn had been loud enough to start dogs barking. It was also loud enough to make a few neighbours look out of their windows.

Some of them saw a figure slipping through the shadows. A tall woman.

Lady Dedlock was a tall woman.

But then so was Hortense.

The inspector had the maid's room searched. There, the policeman found two more letters. Both of them said, 'Lady Dedlock, murderer'. Just like the one at Mr Tulkinghorn's office.

Inspector Bucket arrested Hortense. She quickly admitted that she had murdered Mr Tulkinghorn. She had killed the lawyer after an argument over money. Afterwards, she threw the pistol in the river and tried to make

Lady Dedlock look guilty.

But where was Lady Dedlock?

Esther Summerson and Inspector
Bucket began to search for her.
Sir Leicester was too upset to join
them. Lady Dedlock shouldn't have
worried. Her husband was not
angry when he heard her secrets.
He loved Lady Deadlock dearly and
wanted her back.

Esther, too, was desperate to see
her new-found mother.

But it was not to be.

When they found Lady Dedlock,
she was lying by the gate of the

poor people's cemetery. The place where her first love, Captain James Hawdon, was buried. Her arm was wrapped round an iron bar as if she had been trying to get through to join him.

Esther's eyes filled with tears. Her mother, Lady Deadlock, was dead.

THE END OF JARNDYCE AND JARNDYCE

Life carried on, and one day it brought the news that the Jarndyce and Jarndyce case was finally finished. It had been going on for so long that no one had expected it ever to end. Now, finally, it was over.

As it happened, Esther, Ada, Richard and Mr Jarndyce were there to see the end. Richard had gone against John Jarndyce's warning and become involved in the case.

His health suffered, and he grew pale and thin. His friends worried a lot about him.

One morning, they all went to the courthouse in London. As they arrived, they were met by a huge crowd. There were a lot of lawyers with wigs on. They were all in a good mood, chatting and joking.

'What's going on?' John Jarndyce asked one of the lawyers.

'Haven't you heard?' he answered. 'It's Jarndyce and Jarndyce.'

'What about Jarndyce and Jarndyce?' said Richard eagerly. His eyes shone. His voice was hoarse.

'Why, it's over,' said another lawyer.

'All finished,' said a third.

'What's the judgement?' said Richard.

'There's no judgement.'

'Why not?' asked Mr Jarndyce.

By now, more people were streaming out of the courthouse. They were carting out great bundles of paper. Bags of paper, sacks of paper, boxes of paper.

'There is no money left,' said one of the lawyers, laughing. 'It's all gone.'

'Gone where?' said Ada.

'Well,' said the lawyer, 'It costs money to produce all this paper and to pay people like us, you know.'

'And now it's all gone,' said John Jarndyce.

For many, many years the case of Jarndyce and Jarndyce had taken over people's lives. And sometimes it had ruined them. Richard had been saved in time.

With the court case gone,
Richard could move on with
his life. Soon, he and Ada were
married with a baby boy.

Esther went on to have a happy
life too. She got married to a man
that she loved and had children.
She had met Lady Dedlock only
twice, but she kept the memory
of her in her heart. And she
always carried with her the white
handkerchief. It was thin and faded
now but the corner still had the
letters H.B. on it.

Her mother's initials.

Charles Dickens

Charles Dickens was born in Portsmouth in 1812. Like many of the characters he wrote about, his family were poor and his childhood was difficult. As an adult, he became known around the world for his books. He is remembered as one of the most important writers of his time.

Illustrations by
Jon Davis

A pirate, an old elephant, a witch in shorts, a bear on a bicycle, an ugly cat, adorable children, whatever you want…. John Davies likes to paint while thinking of characters and plots with a child's mind. Tools don't care.

BLEAK HOUSE

초판 1쇄 발행 2023년 6월 27일

글 찰스 디킨스 | 그림 존 데이비스

ISBN 979-11-6581-431-1 (74840)
ISBN 979-11-6581-418-2 (세트)

＊잘못 만들어진 책은 구입하신 곳에서 바꾸어 드립니다.

발행처 주식회사 스푼북 | **발행인** 박상희 | **총괄** 김남원
편집 김선영·박선정·김선혜·권새미 | **디자인** 조혜진·김광휘 | **마케팅** 손준연·이성호·구혜지
출판신고 2016년 11월 15일 제2017-000267호
주소 (03993) 서울시 마포구 월드컵북로 6길 88-7 ky21빌딩 2층
전화 02-6357-0050(편집) 02-6357-0051(마케팅)
팩스 02-6357-0052 | 전자우편 book@spoonbook.co.kr

제품명 Bleak House
제조자명 주식회사 스푼북 | **제조국명** 대한민국 | **전화번호** 02-6357-0050
주소 (03993) 서울시 마포구 월드컵북로6길 88-7 ky21빌딩 2층
제조년월 2023년 6월 27일 | **사용연령** 8세 이상
※ KC마크는 이 제품이 공통안전기준에 적합하였음을 의미합니다.

⚠ 주 의

아이들이 모서리에 다치지
않게 주의하세요.